© 1995 Tormont Publications Inc., 338 St. Antoine Street East, Montreal, Quebec, Canada H2Y 1A3, Tel.: (514) 954-1441, Fax: (514) 954-5086
Illustrations: Zapp Graphic Design: Zapp Text: Carol Krenz
ISBN 2-89429-670-3   Printed in U.S.A.

THE LITTLE MERMAID

ONCE upon a time, a little Mermaid named Coraline lived at the bottom of the sea with her three sisters and her father, the King of the Ocean. They lived in a splendid palace made of corals, shells and pearls, and the girls played happily with the fish and sea horses.

Coraline had the most beautiful singing voice. Even the jellyfish, who usually ignored mermaids, listened to her songs.

Though Coraline loved her world of peaceful blue water, she longed to swim to the surface to see the sky.

"I want to see the sun, the stars and the moon," she told her father. "And I especially want to see humans. They must have such interesting lives."

"When you're fifteen, according to our customs, you may swim to the top of the ocean and see these wonders," he told her.

CORALINE waited impatiently. Her sisters turned fifteen and made their voyage to the air.

"What's it like?" asked Coraline.

And they told her about black rocks and the warm sun.

"We saw sea gulls, too. Their cry is very sad. Perhaps they see too many sailors drown," said her sisters.

Finally the day came for Coraline's visit. She hadn't slept the night before. She was too excited.

She broke through the surface of the foam and smiled up at the sun. It was the most beautiful sight she had ever seen. From her perch on a black rock, she saw a sandy beach. Huge palm trees swayed in the invisible wind and the air smelled crisp and clean.

JUST as the sun was about to set, a ship appeared in the distance and dropped anchor. Now Coraline pricked up her ears to hear the crew speak.

"Happy Birthday, Your Highness," the sailors shouted to a handsome young Prince who was the ship's Captain.

When Coraline saw this regal man, she wished she could speak to him and give him her birthday wishes too. But humans were afraid of mermaids.

The birthday party on the ship was a merry sight. Tiny colored lanterns twinkled red, blue and gold and there was much dancing and laughter. The party was so noisy that the men didn't hear the winds begin to howl.

Soon a raging storm blew up, with fierce black waves.

"LOOK OUT!" Coraline screamed, but no one heard her. The ship pitched and tossed sickeningly and then it capsized. Everyone, including the Prince, was washed overboard.

Coraline dove into the water and quickly swam to him. The Prince was unconscious, so she held his head above the water. She stayed with him all night as the storm raged and the foam churned.

By morning the storm had blown itself out. Coraline pushed the Prince with the last of her strength onto dry land. Then she covered him with her long hair to keep him warm. She sang sweetly to him and stroked his forehead. She prayed he would soon awake.

SUDDENLY, a beautiful woman appeared on the beach. Coraline grew frightened and slipped behind a rock to hide.

"Andre!" the woman cried upon seeing the Prince. "We thought we had lost you forever!"

He opened his eyes. Coraline's sweet song still echoed in his memory. "You have the most beautiful voice," he whispered. "Thank you for saving me."

"I didn't save you, my Prince. Perhaps it was the waves. But I'm glad I found you," the beautiful woman smiled. "Now let me help you back to the palace. Your family will be so thankful that you're alive! If you can't walk, lean on me, Andre."

Slowly the woman led the Prince up the beach away from the sea.

Coraline slipped under the waves and swam home. She wept when she realized how much she loved Prince Andre.

"Where have you been, Coraline? What were you doing up there?" her sisters asked.

But Coraline said nothing. She hurried to her bedroom and refused to eat for three days. She was so miserable that she couldn't speak.

"Daughter, why do you weep all day and night?" asked the King.

"Oh, Father! Please forgive me, but I wish to become a human. I am in love with a man. I must be with him!" Coraline cried.

"Coraline, we don't belong in the human world," he explained.

"Still, I must go to him!" Coraline insisted. But no one would help. At last, she decided her only hope was to visit the Witch of the Ocean.

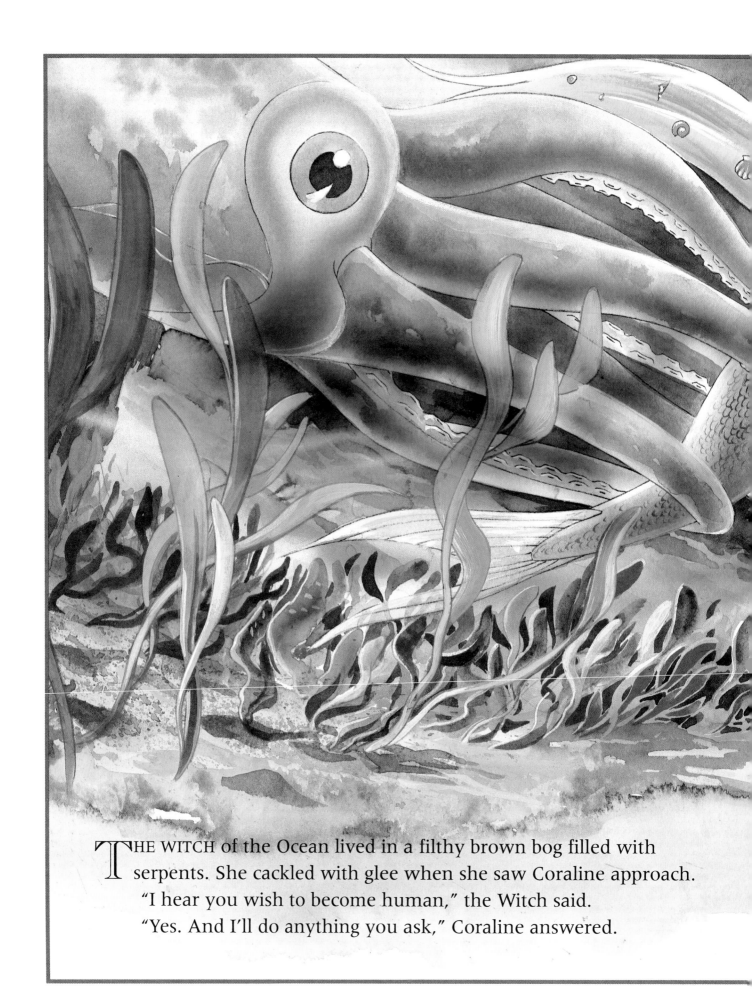

THE WITCH of the Ocean lived in a filthy brown bog filled with serpents. She cackled with glee when she saw Coraline approach.

"I hear you wish to become human," the Witch said.

"Yes. And I'll do anything you ask," Coraline answered.

"Can you stand the pain of being cut in two?" asked the Witch.
"If you take on legs and surrender your tail, that's what it will feel like."
"I'll take any pain if I can walk on dry land," Coraline said.

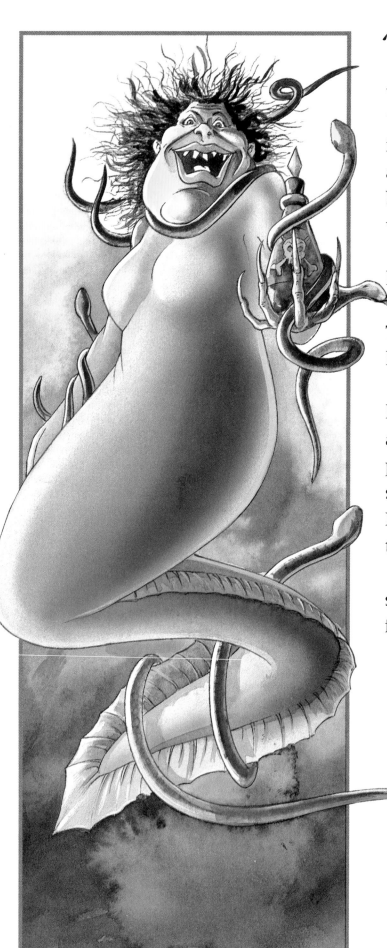

"IN EXCHANGE for legs, you will have to give away your pretty voice," the Witch continued. "You will never speak again. And if your young man marries another instead, you can never be a mermaid again, and your life will end."

Coraline nodded quietly, her heart so filled with fear and hope that she could not speak. Then she took the vial of black liquid from the Witch.

Coraline said goodbye to her watery world, to her sisters and father and her sweet playmates, the sea horses. And she swam up to the beach by the Prince's palace. Then she drank the magic potion.

Suddenly, a searing pain sliced through her tail and she fainted.

THIS time it was Prince Andre who rescued Coraline. He was walking on the shore when he discovered a beautiful girl wearing a most unusual dress of shining scales. Her face glowed when she saw him.

As Coraline walked with the Prince to the palace, she noticed everyone pointing at her in surprise. They asked her questions but she could not answer them. Her voice was gone forever. So she smiled instead and leaned on the Prince's arm.

EVERY step Coraline took was sheer torture, but she walked bravely.

"Look at her dress!" said the ladies of the Court. "How did she make it? And her hair hangs in strange waves down to her ankles. Doesn't she know that's dangerous and she might trip?" they wondered.

"She looks a little too exotic," sniffed one woman. "There are cockle and mussel shells on her toes!"

Coraline became the object of much idle gossip and curiosity.

BUT PRINCE Andre invited her to stay as his guest for as long as she wished, and the royal court soon grew accustomed to her strange ways. For example, the only food Coraline ate was seaweed salad, which she picked at delicately with her fingers.

Weeks flew by and Coraline happily spent her time with Prince Andre. The Prince was extremely kind to her. He treated her like a little sister. But Prince Andre's thoughts of love were elsewhere.

"SOMEONE rescued me after I nearly drowned," he told Coraline one evening. "Hers were the first eyes I saw when I came to. She was only here on a visit, but I miss her."

After that, Coraline crept out of the palace into the moonlight each night and listened to the ocean. She felt so lonely that her heart nearly broke. She knew the Prince would never think of marrying her, no matter what her eyes might say to him.

"I will stay with him for as long as I can," she decided. But she knew that when he married, she would have to die.

The beautiful woman arrived finally for a state visit. It was obvious that she loved the Prince as much as he loved her.

"Clarisse, meet my sweet little sister, a stranger who cannot speak," the Prince said. "We must always look after her."

ONE MORNING, wedding bells rang out through the kingdom. Prince Andre and Clarisse were marrying at last. Poor Coraline could not bear to see them. So she pretended to be sick in bed.

But soon, curiosity got the better of her and she joined the wedding party on the Prince's new ship.

Everyone was celebrating. But when Prince Andre asked Coraline to dance, he saw that she was troubled.

"What's wrong, little sister?" he asked with alarm.

Coraline shook her head as if to say, "Why, nothing at all." And she smiled brightly until the Prince smiled back.

Then when no one was looking, she hurried away from the crowd and climbed into a rowboat. There, no one could see her despair.

SUDDENLY, from her hiding place, she heard her sisters' voices calling, "Coraline! Coraline!"

Coraline rowed quickly out to see them. Their reunion brought happy tears.

"We've come to save you!" they said. "We sold our hair to the Witch for a magic knife. If you kill the Prince before dawn, you can become a mermaid again and come home to us."

Coraline took their knife and waved good-bye. She knew she would never use it. Instead, she waited until past midnight to creep into the bedchamber of the Prince and his Bride.

They slept with their arms around each other in peaceful slumber. They were so beautiful that Coraline kissed their foreheads. Then she left softly on tiptoe.

WHEN dawn broke, Coraline tossed the knife overboard. Then, with a last look at the mortal world, she threw herself into the sea.

Suddenly she felt herself rising up out of the water, surrounded by pretty Fairies with delicate wings.

"We are the Fairies of the Air," they told her. "We help humans in trouble. And we take among us only those mermaids who have shown kindness to mortal beings."

Coraline looked down at the Prince's ship and her eyes filled with tears of love.

"Come, Coraline," the Fairies said. "Your tears have turned to dewdrops to nourish the flowers."

Coraline flew away with the Fairies. And she lives to this day to help young and old who are good of heart.

THE
Twelve Dancing Princesses

ONCE upon a time, there was a King who had twelve beautiful
daughters. Every evening he kissed his daughters goodnight, but in the
morning when he came to awaken them, he saw that their new shoes had
holes in them.

And the Princesses were always so tired. He tried locking their door at night but each morning their shoes were worn out nevertheless. Where his daughters went and how they left their room was a mystery that no one could solve.

FINALLY, the King ordered signs posted on every tree in the kingdom. The signs read: "Any man who can discover where the Royal Princesses go at night will be able to choose one of them for a wife. He will have three nights to try to solve the mystery. But if he fails his mission, he will lose his head."

FROM far and wide they came, handsome young men eager for the hand of a Princess in marriage! They were locked into the antechamber with the Princesses. The Princesses gave them some wine. It was so strong and the seat was so comfortable that each young man slept through the three nights.

Soon no man was willing to try his luck and risk losing his head!

ONE day a soldier, new to the city, heard about the King's challenge. On his way to the castle he met an old woman and told her of his ambition.

"Don't drink the royal wine and keep your wits about you," she advised wisely.

"Here, lad," the old woman smiled, "take this cloak with you. It will make you invisible so that you can follow the Princesses wherever they go."

THE Princesses were not at all worried that they would be discovered. The oldest smiled at this new soldier and offered him ruby red wine. He pretended to drink, but instead he poured the wine into a nearby plant. Then he pretended to sleep and snored quite believably.

"HURRY, we're late," said the oldest Princess and they put on their fine dresses and jewels and newest pairs of dancing shoes.
But then the youngest said, "I have an uneasy feeling. Perhaps we shouldn't go to the ball tonight."

"Don't be silly, he's fast asleep like all the others," the oldest one replied, and she tapped three times on her bedpost.

Slowly the bed sank into the floor, revealing a long marble staircase.

THE soldier immediately threw on his cloak and raced down the stairs after the Princesses. In his haste he stepped on the dress of the youngest.

"Someone stepped on my gown!" she cried.

"Nonsense," said the oldest. "You probably caught it on a nail."

THE stairs brought them to an enchanted forest filled with trees of gold. The soldier snapped off a twig to keep as proof of his journey.

"What was that?" the youngest Princess cried.

"Just the wind rustling the trees," the oldest Princess answered.

They passed silver and diamond trees, and the soldier snapped those twigs too. Each time, the youngest Princess cried out in alarm and looked behind her. But no one paid any attention to her worries.

SOON they came to a magnificent blue lake with twelve huge swan boats waiting at the shore. In each boat was a handsome young Prince. The soldier hopped into the last boat and sat with the youngest Princess.

"Goodness," she said to her young Prince, "the boat feels awfully heavy tonight."

"Yes," he agreed, "I can hardly move it. And it's strangely warm, too."

THE boats soon brought them to a beautiful castle with a magnificent ballroom. There was fine food and music and the twelve Princesses danced well into the early morning until they were quite exhausted. The soldier danced when they danced and ate the fine food.

FINALLY, by dawn, the Princesses had danced their shoes to tatters, and they prepared to return home. The soldier took the first boat back and raced ahead up the staircase. When the Princesses checked on him, he appeared to be fast asleep.

The soldier followed them for three nights. On the third night, he stole a pure gold wine goblet to show the King where he had been.

AFTER the third night, the King asked the soldier, "Do you know where my daughters go at night?"

"They dance until dawn with twelve young Princes in an enchanted world with gold, silver and diamond trees," the soldier replied.

The King found this hard to believe, but the young man showed the royal court the twigs he had stolen from the trees, and the golden goblet.

"Is this true?" the King asked his daughters.

"Yes, Papa," they answered.

"WELL, young man, it seems you have succeeded where everyone else has failed. And now you may choose one of my daughters for a wife," the King said.

"I would be honored all the days of my life if I could have the hand of your eldest daughter," the soldier declared.

The eldest Princess smiled shyly at the soldier and the couple soon married. As for the eleven younger Princesses, they all found charming husbands of their own. And so the twelve Princesses lived happily for the rest of their days.